# SNOOPY AND CHARLIE BROWN

## THE PEANUTS MOVIE

*by SCHULZ*

# THE STORY OF THE FILM

D1150125

PUFFIN BOOKS

UK | USA | Canada | Ireland | Australia
India | New Zealand | South Africa

Puffin Books is part of the Penguin Random House group of companies
whose addresses can be found at global.penguinrandomhouse.com.

puffinbooks.com

First published 2015
001

Printed in the United Kingdom

A CIP catalogue record for this book is available from the British Library

ISBN: 978 – 0 – 141 – 36742 – 2

# SNOOPY AND CHARLIE BROWN

## THE PEANUTS MOVIE

*by Schulz*

# THE STORY OF THE FILM

Peanuts created by
## CHARLES M. SCHULZ

PUFFIN

# THE PEANUTS

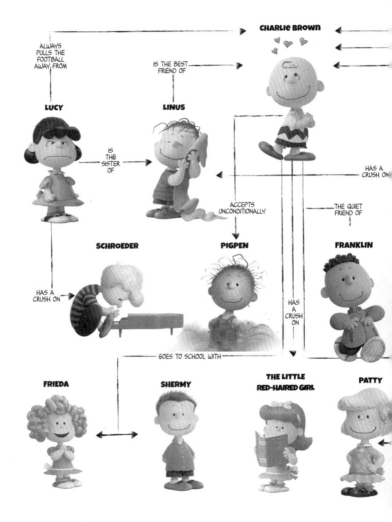

CHARLIE BROWN

ALWAYS PULLS THE FOOTBALL AWAY FROM

IS THE BEST FRIEND OF

LUCY

IS THE SISTER OF

LINUS

HAS A CRUSH ON

ACCEPTS UNCONDITIONALLY

THE QUIET FRIEND OF

SCHROEDER

PIGPEN

FRANKLIN

HAS A CRUSH ON

HAS A CRUSH ON

GOES TO SCHOOL WITH

FRIEDA

SHERMY

THE LITTLE RED-HAIRED GIRL

PATTY

# FAMILY TREE

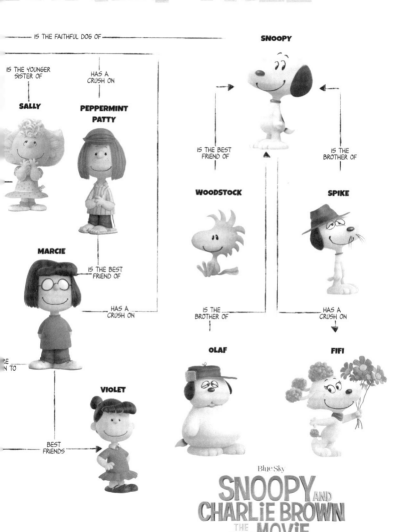

IS THE FAITHFUL DOG OF

SNOOPY

IS THE YOUNGER SISTER OF

**SALLY**

HAS A CRUSH ON

**PEPPERMINT PATTY**

IS THE BEST FRIEND OF

IS THE BROTHER OF

**WOODSTOCK**

**SPIKE**

**MARCIE**

IS THE BEST FRIEND OF

HAS A CRUSH ON

IS THE BROTHER OF

HAS A CRUSH ON

**OLAF**

**FIFI**

**VIOLET**

BEST FRIENDS

# CHAPTER ONE

Charlie Brown is always last to wake up. It's dark. It's cold. It's a school day. But, as he slowly opens his eyes on THIS day, something feels different.

He can hear his little sister, Sally, on the phone downstairs.

"Snow day? Snow day!" she says. "No school today?"

Lifting his head from the pillow, Charlie Brown thinks maybe today won't be so bad after all!

As he struggles to get dressed, he hears voices outside.

"Hurry up – let's go!"
"Race you to the pond!"

Charlie Brown grabs his hat and rushes outside. The pavement is empty. Everyone has gone.

BUT . . .

He has a thought as a silent gust of snowy wind blows by.

"This could be the day! A new kite, a gentle breeze – it all feels just right!" he says with excitement.

Out in the field, Charlie Brown holds the string of his new kite firmly and runs as fast as he can.

"It's in the air! It's FLYING!" he shouts to his friends who are playing on the ice pond at the bottom of the hill.

The kite IS flying . . . but so is Charlie Brown! He is so busy watching the kite that he doesn't notice the string getting caught on his foot. He trips and slides all the way down the hill on his front.

"Watch out!" he shouts to his friends. "Coming through!"

But Lucy is too far away to hear him.

"And now for my famous triple axel!" she says confidently – just as Charlie Brown sends her hurtling across the ice.

But it's much worse for Charlie Brown. He spins out of control off the ice and ends up hanging upside down in the Kite-Eating Tree.

"You blockhead!" yells Lucy. "What kind of person tries to fly a kite in the middle of winter?! Don't you ever give up? You will never get that kite to fly. Why? Because you're Charlie Brown!"

"It's going to be a long winter," says Charlie Brown with a sigh.

Suddenly the sound of a truck's horn sends the gang running to peer over a high wooden fence that runs along the field. It's a moving truck!

"Hey, there's a new kid moving in!" says Franklin as they all try to get a look over the fence.

"I hope he will appreciate my natural beauty," says Lucy.

"I hope he believes in the Great Pumpkin!" adds Linus excitedly.

"I just hope he's never heard of me and all my failures," mutters Charlie Brown sadly. "It's not often you get the chance to start again with a clean slate. This time things will be different."

# CHAPTER TWO

The next morning, Charlie Brown and his friends walk to school together. Even Snoopy is with them.

"No dogs allowed!" announces Franklin as the school door closes on Snoopy's gloomy face.

When Charlie Brown gets to his classroom, it is in chaos and everyone is chatting at the same time. They all want to know about the new kid. As he walks to his desk, Charlie Brown stops to talk to his good friend Linus who is playing with something cool. It looks like a plane.

"It's my turn for show-and-tell today," Linus explains. "This is the plane flown by the Red Baron – the most famous aviator of the Great War."

As Charlie Brown reaches over and starts to spin the propeller, they are startled to hear the sound of an engine starting up. Suddenly the little red plane is in the air!

"Duck, Linus, duck!" shouts Charlie Brown as the plane whips over their heads and out of the window.

Just then, the classroom door opens and their teacher, Miss Othmar, walks in . . . and someone else is following just behind her.

It's the new kid. And she has beautiful red hair.

Charlie Brown's heart starts to beat faster, his eyes glaze over and his head suddenly seems full of cotton wool.

Charlie Brown is in love.

As the Little Red-Haired Girl takes her seat, the teacher hands out test papers. How is Charlie Brown ever going to be able to concentrate?

Later, Charlie Brown sees the Little Red-Haired Girl get up to hand in her test. As she steps away from her desk, her special feathered pink pencil falls on to the floor . . . and rolls away . . . and stops . . . right in front of him.

This is destiny.

Charlie Brown reaches down and picks up the pencil. As he admires it, he notices there are tiny nibble marks all over it.

"She nibbles her pencil like me!" he marvels.

# CHAPTER THREE

Charlie Brown feels like he is walking on air. He can't stop smiling. His heart is pounding in his chest. His knees are a little weak.

And the Little Red-Haired Girl has no idea he is even alive.

By the time Charlie Brown steps off the school bus that afternoon he has made a decision. A big one. He is going to go to her house and give her a gift: a flower he picked. It's going to be perfect.

"I can't believe I am about to talk to the Little Red-Haired Girl," he says to himself as he slowly walks along the pavement to her door.

Charlie Brown nervously reaches for the doorbell . . . and almost pushes it. But he is NEVER going to be brave enough to speak to her.

Feeling glum, he drags his feet as he goes to see Lucy. She is sitting in her booth, the words "Psychiatric Help. 5 cents" in big letters on the front.

"I need your advice," he begins. "There's a girl I'd like to impress. I just need to know the secret to winning her heart."

Lucy pulls out a mirror from underneath her booth and holds it up to Charlie Brown's face. "Look into this mirror," she says bossily. "A classic failure face. Do you think girls like failures, Charlie Brown?"

Charlie Brown is staring hard at his face in the mirror. "Well, no . . ." he replies quietly, his self-confidence slowly ebbing away.

She pulls out a book and hands it to him. It's called *10 Ways to Become a Winner.*

"If you really want to impress girls," she says, "you need to show them you're a winner! I don't mean you personally," she continues. "We all know you couldn't possibly win anything, Charlie Brown!"

Back home in his bedroom, Charlie Brown is trying hard to concentrate on his book, but there is the most terrible noise coming from the living room. Sally is standing in the middle of a pile of boxes dressed as a rodeo rider.

"What are you doing?" he asks with a sigh, noticing she is riding a horse . . . which is really a mop, with a nose . . . that is really a paper bag.

"I'm going to be a rodeo star in the big talent show!" she yells. "Yee-haw!"

A crazy idea begins whizzing round Charlie Brown's head as he watches Sally twirling her lasso. "Win the talent show," he says to himself. "Now that's a great idea! This is just what Lucy was talking about!"

Rushing back up to his bedroom, Charlie Brown knows he can do this! Brimming with excitement, and whistling for his assistant, Snoopy, he pulls out his magic set and gets practising.

There's a lot of work to be done, but they make a great team.

# CHAPTER FOUR

The night of the talent show comes round and Charlie Brown watches from backstage as the hall begins to fill up and the stage lights dip. He knows the Little Red-Haired Girl is in the audience.

Charlie Brown is feeling confident in his tuxedo and top hat. He tells himself he has great tricks to perform and he has practised hard. NOTHING can go wrong tonight.

"I have a really good feeling that tonight she will see the new Charlie Brown," he whispers to Snoopy.

He watches Sally as she leaps on to the stage. "Ride 'em, cowgirl!" she yells from her cardboard rodeo set.

As Charlie Brown begins to move his props into position for his magic act, he looks up at the sound of laughter coming from the audience. Was Sally's act meant to be funny? He goes to find out what's happening onstage . . . and he doesn't like what he sees. The audience is laughing as Sally tries to lasso a cardboard cow. She is looking nervous.

"Hey, that's not a real cow," calls Lucy.

The music comes to a sudden stop when the cardboard head of Sally's cow falls to the ground.

Charlie Brown feels terrible for Sally. From where he is standing, he can see she has tears in her eyes.

Without further thought, Charlie Brown joins Sally onstage and pretends to be a cow. He knows in some part of his mind that he must look ridiculous, but he has to help his little sister.

"Rope me! Moo!" he calls to her, smiling with encouragement. Sally's eyes light up as she races after him across the stage.

"I'm gonna get you!" she shouts, quite liking this new turn in her performance. "Woo hoo!"

Now Sally's act has been saved, Charlie Brown wants it to be over. He knows the Little Red-Haired Girl must be watching, so bravely he allows himself to be lassoed and hopes that will be an end to it. But Sally is really loving being a cowgirl now.

"My name is Calamity Sally," she yells. "The best lasso-roping cowgirl in this here town!" Without warning, she picks Charlie Brown up, throws him down on his side and wraps the rope all round him. Now he knows he definitely looks ridiculous.

"Thanks, big brother," she whispers as the crowd goes wild and the flashbulbs pop.

# CHAPTER FIVE

**C**harlie Brown was not a winner. But he could be. He knows he can. Pacing up and down the living room, concentrating hard on *10 Ways to Become a Winner*, he doesn't even hear the phone ringing.

"Your girlfriend's on the phone," Sally calls out to him.

*It can't be*, he thinks. *Phoning me? The Little Red-Haired Girl?*

But it's only Peppermint Patty, and Charlie Brown tries not to feel a bit let down as she tells him all about the Winter Dance, which is taking place in a few weeks' time. Charlie Brown sighs. Why would he want to go to the Winter Dance anyway?

"Marcie put me on the refreshment committee," she chatters on. "And I signed you up to make the cupcakes."

Poor Charlie Brown. This is getting worse and worse.

That night, dragging his feet up the stairs to bed, Charlie Brown thinks he can hear faint music. Peering out of the window, he sees a light on in the Little Red-Haired Girl's house. Although it's dark and snow is falling heavily, he can just make out the figure of a girl with a cloud of whirling red hair dancing around the room. She looks like an angel and he can hardly breathe as he watches her.

The next morning, Sally wonders why the whole house seems to be shaking. Music is thumping out of Charlie Brown's bedroom and every so often there is a huge CRASH!

"Turn it down! What's going on in there?" she yells, flinging open the door to his room. Sally is surprised, and a little bit nervous, to see her big brother doing a crazy out-of-control dance . . . with a mop for a partner. As she watches, he whips around the room, knocking the lamp off his nightstand.

"She likes to dance!" he calls over his shoulder by way of explanation as he crashes into his bed.

Suddenly Snoopy is there, too. *The noise must have been really bad to wake that beagle up*, thinks Sally as she shakes her head and walks away. But Snoopy is here to help . . . and he's brought props.

Snoopy lays some footprints on the floor in a simple pattern, then encourages Charlie Brown to try the steps.

"One, two, three. One, two, three," whispers Charlie Brown under his breath as he begins to master the technique.

Snoopy moves around the room, adjusting Charlie Brown's arm here and his foot there, until the dance begins to come together.

# CHAPTER SIX

The Winter Dance is tonight and the school gym has been transformed. There are balloons and streamers along the walls, and coloured lights bounce off a spinning mirror ball.

The guys nervously tap their feet on one side of the room . . . while the girls do the same on the other.

"Why isn't anyone dancing?" shouts Sally over the music. Linus hears her voice and knows what's coming. He tries to hide himself under his blanket but it's no good. Sally has seen him and pulls him on to the dance floor. Gradually, the others start to shuffle after them, and soon the dance is in full swing.

From outside, Charlie Brown can hear the music getting louder as he makes his way towards the gym, carrying his cupcakes. Snoopy is following close behind – he doesn't like to miss out on a party, and he is a great dancer.

"I couldn't have done it without you," says Charlie Brown warmly to his four-legged dance coach. He is practising dance moves in his head, so is surprised to look down and see his cupcakes have ALL GONE! *Snoopy looks very innocent*, he thinks to himself. *Just a pity about the frosting all over his face.*

Charlie Brown arrives just in time – the girls' dance competition is about to start. Music pounds, and Charlie Brown catches his breath as he sees the Little Red-Haired Girl take her turn, her friends all cheering and whooping as she goes.

"Listen to that noise," says DJ Franklin. "I think we know who our winner is!"

Charlie Brown's smile is enormous. The Little Red-Haired Girl has won!

"And now it's the gentlemen's turn," continues DJ Franklin. "Who will be joining our lovely winning lady for the final dance of the night?"

Charlie Brown's heart thumps as the music starts up again and he gets ready to take his turn on the dance floor.

"This is it," he mutters under his breath. "It's now or never."

Snoopy is finishing his dance and the cheers ring in Charlie Brown's ears. It's his turn next. With a deep breath, he begins, performing the dance just as Snoopy taught him. After a few seconds, he is sure the cheers are getting a little louder. Glancing up, he sees that he's right. Everyone is smiling and clapping.

It's going to be OK! He can just about hear Franklin through the cheers, saying, "It looks like we may have a winner here!"

Just as Charlie Brown is close enough to the Little Red-Haired Girl to almost touch her, he slips and falls backwards. But worse happens: his shoe flies off and sails up into the air.

Charlie Brown watches, in what feels like slow motion, as it hits something on the ceiling, up among the balloons and streamers. Charlie Brown's shoe has hit a fire sprinkler!

As cold water sprays down, soaking the dancers in their colourful party clothes, people start to run from the gym.

Charlie Brown is left standing in the soggy gym, surrounded by ruined decorations.

"This is not how it was supposed to end," he says. Charlie Brown feels like his heart is breaking.

As Charlie Brown is standing there, a small voice says, "Hello." It's the Little Red-Haired Girl. She's still there and she is looking right at him!

Charlie Brown blushes. "Why would you want to talk to me? I'm just a failure," he mutters, looking down at his feet.

She walks over to him and begins to tell Charlie Brown how much she admires him. "You showed compassion for your sister at the talent show, and here at the dance you were brave yet funny. So you see, when I look at you, I don't see a failure at all. I see a friend."

The Little Red-Haired Girl wants to be his friend, despite all his mistakes. She likes him because he never gave up. Charlie Brown can't stop smiling!

It feels really good to be Charlie Brown.

**THE END**

## MEET THE PEANUTS GANG!

### CHARLIE BROWN

Charlie Brown tries his best at everything
he does, but it doesn't always go to plan.
Despite his own troubles, he's always a
good big brother, a devoted pet owner
and all-around Good ol' Charlie Brown.

### SNOOPY

Snoopy is Charlie Brown's dog and the
neighbourhood's favourite beagle. A legend
in his own mind, Snoopy can take to the skies,
rule the college campus or write another
unpublished manuscript.

### WOODSTOCK

Woodstock is Snoopy's best friend and confidant.
His fluttering doesn't get him very far!
But, luckily for him, he always lands on
Snoopy's doghouse!

## LINUS

Linus is Charlie Brown's best friend.
He is the voice of reason and philosophy
in the neighbourhood.

## SALLY

Sally is Charlie Brown's little sister
and believes the world owes
her an explanation.

## LUCY

Lucy is known for being crabby and bossy.
She can often be found dispensing advice
from her 5-cent psychiatrist's booth.

## SCHROEDER

Schroeder is devoted to his
music, always improving
his craft and aspiring to the
greatness of his idol, Beethoven.

## PEPPERMINT PATTY

Peppermint Patty loves sports and she's
up for any challenge . . . except studying!
She is also known as 'Sir'.

## MARCIE

Marcie is Peppermint Patty's best friend.
But they are complete opposites!
Marcie is the smart one of the
group, but terrible at sports!

## PIGPEN

An archeologist in the making,
if there's a pile of dirt around,
Pigpen will be in it!

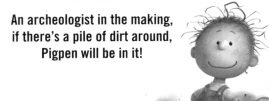

## FRANKLIN

Franklin is Charlie Brown's
thoughtful friend and confidant.

## LITTLE RED-HAIRED GIRL

When the Little Red-Haired Girl moves
into the neighbourhood, Charlie Brown's
world is turned upside down. If only he
can find the courage to talk to her.

# CHARLIE BROWN'S CODE

Charlie Brown has some great advice for you!
But there's a problem – the message has got
all muddled up! Can you use the code wheel
to find the solution?

## CHARLIE BROWN'S CODE

4 15 14 ' 20 / 6 15 18 7 5 20 : /
14 5 22 5 18 / 7 9 22 5 / 21 16!

\_\_\_ ' \_ _____:

\_\_\_\_\_ \_\_\_\_ \_\_!

# SNOOPY'S FAVOURITES

Lots of Snoopy's favourite things are hidden in this word search – can you find them all?

SUPPERTIME   COOKIES   ADVENTURE

FOOD   DOGHOUSE   SLEEP

FLYING   WOODSTOCK  PIZZA

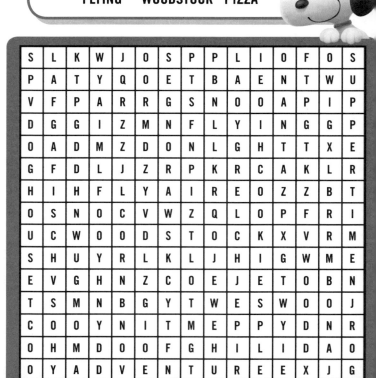

| S | L | K | W | J | O | S | P | P | L | I | O | F | O | S |
|---|---|---|---|---|---|---|---|---|---|---|---|---|---|---|
| P | A | T | Y | Q | O | E | T | B | A | E | N | T | W | U |
| V | F | P | A | R | R | G | S | N | O | O | A | P | I | P |
| D | G | G | I | Z | M | N | F | L | Y | I | N | G | G | P |
| O | A | D | M | Z | D | O | N | L | G | H | T | T | X | E |
| G | F | D | L | J | Z | R | P | K | R | C | A | K | L | R |
| H | I | H | F | L | Y | A | I | R | E | O | Z | Z | B | T |
| O | S | N | O | C | V | W | Z | Q | L | O | P | F | R | I |
| U | C | W | O | O | D | S | T | O | C | K | X | V | R | M |
| S | H | U | Y | R | L | K | L | J | H | I | G | W | M | E |
| E | V | G | H | N | Z | C | O | E | J | E | T | O | B | N |
| T | S | M | N | B | G | Y | T | W | E | S | W | O | O | J |
| C | O | O | Y | N | I | T | M | E | P | P | Y | D | N | R |
| O | H | M | D | O | O | F | G | H | I | L | I | D | A | O |
| O | Y | A | D | V | E | N | T | U | R | E | E | X | J | G |

40

## FIND THE FRIENDS

Rearrange the letters in these anagrams
to find the names of ten Peanuts friends.

1. PONYSO _ _ _ _ _ _

2. SOCK DO TWO _ _ _ _ _ _ _ _ _

3. YCLU _ _ _ _

4. SUNIL _ _ _ _ _

5. BOWLER ARCH IN _ _ _ _ _ _ _ _ _ _ _ _

6. LASLY _ _ _ _ _

7. RECORD SHE _ _ _ _ _ _ _ _ _

8. LINK FARN _ _ _ _ _ _ _ _

9. ICE ARM _ _ _ _ _ _

10. PRETTY MAP PEN TIP

_ _ _ _ _ _ _ _ _ _ _ _ _ _

# THE PEANUTS MOVIE QUIZ!

So you think you know the Peanuts gang?
Test your knowledge with this fabulous quiz!

( **1** ) What colour is Linus's blanket?

a) Red
b) Blue
c) Green
d) Spotty

( **2** ) What breed of dog
is Snoopy?

a) Beagle
b) Doberman
c) Labrador
d) Poodle

( **3** ) What does Charlie Brown use
to practise dancing with?

a) Mop
b) Saucepan
c) Lamp
d) Bookcase

**4** What act does Charlie Brown choose to perform at the talent show?

a) Juggling
b) Singing
c) Tap dancing
d) Magic

**5** What vehicle does Snoopy fly?

a) Aeroplane
b) Boat
c) Truck
d) Bicycle

**6** Who plays the piano?

a) Marcie
b) Linus
c) Charlie Brown
d) Schroeder

**7** What dance do the Peanuts gang attend?

a) Autumn
b) Spring
c) Winter
d) Summer

**8** Who offers Charlie Brown advice on girls?

a) Peppermint Patty
b) Marcie
c) Lucy
d) Sally

**9** What's the name of Snoopy's yellow friend?

a) Olaf
b) Charlie Brown
c) Woodstock
d) Sally

**10** What does Marcie call
Peppermint Patty?

a) Mister
b) Baron
c) Lady
d) Sir

**Check the answers on page 47.**
**How many correct answers did you get?**

1 – 3   Good grief! You need to brush up on your
        Peanuts knowledge!

4 – 6   Keep looking up! You are almost there.

7 – 10  Wow! It's clear that you are one of the gang!

# ANSWERS

## page 39

### CHARLIE BROWN'S CODE

**DON'T FORGET:
NEVER GIVE UP!**

## page 40

### SNOOPY'S FAVOURITES

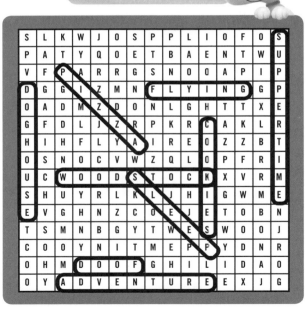

## page 41

### FIND THE FRIENDS

1. SNOOPY
2. WOODSTOCK
3. LUCY
4. LINUS
5. CHARLIE BROWN
6. SALLY
7. SCHROEDER
8. FRANKLIN
9. MARCIE
10. PEPPERMINT PATTY

## pages 42–45

### THE PEANUTS MOVIE QUIZ!

| | | | |
|---|---|---|---|
| 1. | b | 6. | d |
| 2. | a | 7. | c |
| 3. | a | 8. | c |
| 4. | d | 9. | c |
| 5. | a | 10. | d |